T0198939

Light of the Tears

of the

Tears

MS LADI

authorHOUSE®

AuthorHouse™
1663 Liberty Drive
Bloomington, IN 47403
www.authorhouse.com
Phone: 1 (800) 839-8640

Published by AuthorHouse 10/08/2018

ISBN: 978-1-5462-6354-8 (sc)
ISBN: 978-1-5462-6353-1 (e)

Library of Congress Control Number: 2018912010

Print information available on the last page.

Acknowledgment

I would like to thank God for giving me a talent to be able to write the unspoken. I would like to thank my daughter, Diamond, and husband, Johnnie, for being there in my time of need and having faith in me.

I would like to thank my best friend, Naomi.

I would like to thank my big cousin Tasha.

I would like to thank my big brother, Demille, and his wife, Felicia.

I would like to thank my stepmother, Kat.

I would like to thank my publisher and anyone else who was there for me.

Introduction

*T*his book is about the story of abuse, molestation, and running away. The story of abuse is about.

a young girl and her mom being abused by her father and how a certain event set her free. The story of molestation is about a young girl who was molested by her father and how she dealt with the pain.

And the third story is about a young girl running away from home due to the events that were going on at home and how she became free.

Abuse

The sun was shining bright, and the clouds looked like animals in the sky. The wind was blowing slightly while the trees moved to the beat of a distant drum. Hi, my name is Sarah, and I lived in the house with my mom and dad. Living with my parents was very hard at times. We had our good days, but lately it had been very rough. See, my dad liked to drink, and on those days, he took his frustration out on me and my mom. It started when I was five years old. It was not as bad back then; he would slap me around or strike me with a belt. As time grew, the beating would increase to slamming me against the wall and to breaking my arm. Sometimes I would go to school, but most days, I stayed at home with bruise on me.

Well, this is my story. It all started back when I was five. I remember it like it was yesterday. I have a friend by the name of Trina, and we have been friends for as long as I can remember. Trina lives with her mom and dad down the street from me. We do everything together and even get into trouble together. Trina has a big sister by the name of Tasha that is in and out the house all the time. Trina and her sister get along just fine. It's Tasha and her dad that do not see eye to eye sometimes. Tasha lives with her boyfriend most of the time. They treat me like their little sister and are always there when I need them the most.

The first time that my dad put his hands on me, I went to school the next day with welts and bruises all over my back. We were in gym class, and everyone was changing into their gym clothes but me. Trina came over to me and asked me what was wrong. I was too embarrassed to tell her, so I showed her instead. Trina held her hand over her mouth and gasp for air with tears running down her cheek. I made her promise not to tell anyone, not even her sister. She promised and helped me get dressed for gym class.

When school was over, I met Trina in front of the school so that we could ride the bus together. As we found our seat, Trina asked me how long my dad had been beating me. I told her just that one time, and it really was not as bad as it look. As I turned away from Trina, I can see the worry in her eyes like she wanted to do something, but she did not know what to do to help me. We got off the bus and walked three blocks to our house. We said goodbye to each other and went our separate ways.

As I entered the house, I prayed that my dad was in a good mood. My mom was fixing dinner, and my dad was watching TV. I glanced and looked her way, and she just smiled at me. I went and sat next to my dad; as I sat there, I noticed that he was crying. I put my hand on his shoulder and asked him why he was crying. He looked at me and said that he was sorry for hitting me last night and wanted to know if I could forgive him. I put both of my hands around his neck and told him that I forgave him.

I am eight years old now with curly brown hair and a round nose. I have dimples on both cheeks, and I am slim built. I look like any other child that you may see on any old ordinary day.

It all began on a hot and summer day when I came home from school. My mother was sitting in the living room watching TV, and my dad had not come home from work yet. So I was in my room doing my homework when, all of a sudden, I heard a lot of fussing coming from the living area. I got up to see what was going on. As I approached the living room, I saw my dad hitting my mom. I knew where this was going to go, and boy, I did not like it. So I ran back into my room and tried to lock the door, but before I could shut the door all the way, my dad was pushing it open from the other side. As I looked him in his eyes, I saw rage and anger, and I knew what was coming next. As he struck me with his fist, I yelled for my mom, but no luck.

He kept on hitting me in my face, legs, and back. It seemed like this went on for hours. When he was done, he just left without saying anything. I was curled up on the floor crying and yelling for my mom. As I lay there waiting for my mom to come in and check on me, I made a pact with myself that this would be the last time my dad would put his hands on me. I got up off the floor and went toward my door. I put my ear up to it to see if I could hear anything going on in the living room area. It was quiet; all I could hear was the TV playing commercials. So I decided to go to the living room and see about my mom. I opened the room door slowly and quietly, easing out of my room and into the living room. As I looked around the room, I saw my mom lying on the floor in a pool of blood, and there was no sign of my dad. I rushed to my mom's side and checked to see if she was breathing.

My mom was barely breathing with her eyes closed. I rushed to the telephone and called for emergency help. Usually, it has never been this bad—a couple of bruises here and there—but this time, it was awful. As I waited for help to arrive, I prayed to God that everything would be all right. When we got to the hospital, the atmosphere was like water standing still. While waiting for the doctor to come and check out my mom, I saw the moon in the sky as blue as the water on a clear sunny day. It's like peace have come and is taking over the world. It's a very pleasant night. I stood by my mom and told her that everything is going to be all right and that God has a plan for us.

She turned my way, smiled, and said, "I know, baby, I know."

As time passed, we got older and wiser, things were a lot clearer, and we made better decisions. My mom and I ended up moving into a two-bedroom apartment. She was working nights, and she was there in the day to help me with my homework. We got along very well. A couple of months ago, my mom got some very bad news about my dad. I guess he was coming from a bar, and he had been drinking way too much. His car struck a tree, and he was killed instantly. I was very empty inside at the funeral. I really did not know how to feel. My mom cried a lot, but I think it was only due to them being married for about five years.

I loved to go to school; in fact, I was the lead in the play *Romeo and Juliet.* My mom was more excited than I was. She went out and bought me a costume. After the play was over, we went out to eat; it was the most exhilarating night of my life.

So as time went on, Mom got lonely and started to go out and date. I was excited for her; all I wanted was for my mom to be happy. Well, I wish I could say that things were good for us, but it was not. There was one man that did not like kids. So when he was around, I had to leave the house. I would go to the park or to the arcades until late at night. Then there was a guy that wanted me to always sit on his lap. Well, Mom has seen right through that and put him out. I could go on and on about the men she would bring to the house. Most of the time, I would be in my room with the door locked, praying that they would leave and it would just be me and my mom again. I am not trying to be selfish, but it's hard coming from an abusive home to being free.

As time went on, I graduated from middle and high school. I was a straight A honor roll student, and my mom was there by my side with each and every step. My mom ended up marrying a very nice guy that had his own business and had two kids around my age. We grew up happy and healthy, but every now and again, I think back on my life when my dad was here and wondered why he was such a terrible person, that maybe if he had gone to church and prayed more, he would still be here with me. Please do not get me wrong, I still love my dad. I just dislike the way he treated me and my mom.

I grew up and moved out once I graduated from college, and I found a very nice young guy around my age that wanted the same thing as I do. We went to visit my parents often and shared our dreams with them. They wished us the best and made sure we keep God in the midst of it all.

I remember the beating
I remember the pain
Blow after blow after blow
My mind was racing with fear
Thinking what did I do
What didn't I do
Who deserves this
Nobody I say
Nobody at all
I wish I could just
Disappear into the wall
When it was all over
I am covered with bruises
From head to toe
With nothing to say
And nowhere to go

Molestation

The world was spinning around and around like a merry-go-round that I cannot get off. The wind was blowing gently with the softness of the rain. Hi, my name is Gina, and this is my story.

It all started when I was twelve years old. See, I lived with my mom and dad and baby brother. We stayed in an apartment on the south side of the Bronx. I was not a troublemaker. I went to school, got good grades, and did my chores when asked. Well, on this cloudy day, I got out of school and got on the bus to head toward our house. When I got home, my folks were arguing about the bills like always. My baby brother was asleep on the couch, so I went into my room and put my bag away. I went into the kitchen and got myself something to eat. My mom greeted me with a smile, and my dad asked me about my day. I just shrugged my shoulder and said it was a day.

Well, later that night, while everyone was getting ready to go to bed, I noticed the bill for the lights was on the kitchen table. It had red words written on it saying "disconnect notice." I let out a long sigh and headed to bed myself. As I turned over on my bed, I saw a shadow standing over me. I gasped softly and tried to get up to see what it was.

The next thing I know, there was a hand covering my mouth and the other pulling my pants down. I tried to scream, but nothing came out. Tears streamed down my face as I was kicking and trying to pushed him off me. But he was a lot stronger than me, and I realized that this was my dad. I tried to get up, but he kept on pushing me down. Once he got my pants off, he took his off and climbed on top of me. The next thing I remember was a lot of pain. When he was done raping me, he whispered in my ear not to tell anyone or he would harm my mom and little brother and that I deserved what I got. He removed his hand from my mouth, got up, and left. I just lay there in pain and cried.

I woke up earlier than usual, took a shower, and went to school. I was so hurt and still in pain that all I wanted to do was sleep. That's just what I did. I skipped school and went to the park across the school. I found myself a nice shaded tree and lay down underneath it and went to sleep. By the time I woke up, it was getting dark. I looked around, and there were a few people in the park, but no one noticed me. I got up and caught the bus home.

When I got home, my mom was in the kitchen, and my dad was watching TV. I looked for my little brother, and he was on the couch sleeping. It was a relief to me to see that he was not harmed. I went into the kitchen where my mom was fixing my plate for me. I wanted so bad to tell her what had happened, but I was scared that she would not believe me. So I ate in silence. Once I was done eating, I cleaned my plate and went to my room.

I put a chair up to my door for the first couple of weeks, scared that he might come in my room and rape me again. But he was so occupied with other things that he totally forgot that I existed. Until one day, I came home from hanging out in the park, and my parents had been arguing, and it looked like a lick or two had passed. They both looked at me in disgust and kept right on arguing. That night, he came in my room, raped me, and reminded me on what would happen if I told anyone. This went on for two years.

I am fourteen now, and in my mind, this had to stop, but I did not know what to do. So I decided that I would fight and yell until someone heard my cries. I wrote my mom a letter that night explaining to her what has been happening for the last two years of my life. I prayed that she would believe me and take us away from him. But that did not happen; instead, she came in my room and slapped me across the face and said that I was lying. I held my face and tried to explain, but she kept on yelling at me. Not knowing how much more abuse I could take, I ran out of the house and kept running until I could not run anymore. The world seemed to have frozen still for a while, and I was the only one moving. I could see the fine details of the world, and it was amazing. It felt like I have all the power to do what I wanted to with no one watching or caring. Then all of a sudden, I heard a loud horn blowing, and a lady told me to get out the streets.

I did not know what to do next. I did not have any real friends, and I know by now that my dad and mom were not having me back there. So I wandered around the streets for about a week. Then one day, I started to have stomach pains and was not able to keep anything down. I went to the hospital to see what was wrong. As I sat there waiting to be called, I could smell the aroma of the coffee bean brewed and hear people talking in the background. There was a security guard standing next to the door, and people were coming in and out. I sat there scared and not knowing what was going to happen to me.

They called my name, and I followed the nurse to a room at the back. She took my vitals and said that the doctor would be in to see me soon. Then all of a sudden, this lady came in my room and said that she was from the Child Protective Services and asked me where my parents were. I looked at her with tears in my eyes and told her that I did not know. I screamed to her that I was not ever going back there and that she could not make me. She held me and said that everything was going to be all right. The doctor came in, asked me a lot of questions, and told me to go pee in a cup. He said that he wanted to make sure that I did not have any infections. The lady and I talked awhile more, and then the doctor came in and said that I was three months pregnant and dehydrated. They put an IV in my arm and gave me some fluids. The lady came back in the room and asked me who the father was and if my parents knew. I looked at her and told what had been happening to me for the past two years. She sat there with this look on her face like she wanted to kill someone. Once my fluids were done, the nurse gave some literature on prenatal care and shelters in my area. I thanked her and left.

The nice lady followed me out the door and gave me her card and told me to call her if I ever wanted to talk or needed something. I thanked her and walked toward the bus stop to catch a bus to a shelter. When I arrived, the place was empty and scary, and it looked as if nobody was there. I let out a big sigh and went ahead and knocked on the door. A short lady with golden-blond hair by the name of Kim came to the door. She asked me what I wanted. I told her that the lady from the Child Protective Services gave me her name and said that she might have a place for me to stay.

The nice lady showed me around and then had me fill out some paperwork. It was a place for teens that got pregnant and had nowhere to go. She explained to me that later in the program, I was going to have to face my demons. I started to cry and think that's not ever going to happen. As time went by, I settled in and made some new friends. I would read a lot and try to catch up on my homework. I wanted to be as smart as I could when the baby came. Then out of the blue, a few weeks before I was due to have the baby, the social worker came by. She wanted to talk about what I was going to do once the baby was born. I explained to her that I have not given it a thought and asked her of my options. She explained that she thought that the best option for me was to give the baby up for adoption. She went on to say that under my circumstances, that would be the better choice. She must have found someone to take the baby because she handed me papers to sign. I asked her of the other option she had.

The lady looked at me and cleared her throat and said, "Well, you can keep the baby."

My eyes got so moist, and I felt sick to my stomach. I got up, took the papers, and went to my room. I lay there thinking about what just happened, and I started to wonder what it would be like with a child at this young age. I started asking questions to myself. Was I ready? Would I excel at it? Then I told myself that this baby needed a stable home, someone who would give it all the love and nourishment that it needed. So I looked at the papers again and was going to sign them when my water broke. Kim called the ambulance, and I waited outside for them. I was in a little pain, but not much, just a little scared. I did not know what was happening.

We arrived at the hospital. They checked me in and took me to a room upstairs. They put me on a gown and hooked me up to the monitors and put an IV in my hand. The doctor, I guess who was on call, came in and checked to see how far I was. She said that I was at three centimeters and they were going to have me wait it out to see what happens. I lay there wishing my mom was with me. So I called her on the hospital phone, and she picked up the phone saying hello. I said nothing and just started to cry.

She said, "I know that this you, Gina. Please say something."

I started crying harder. My mom said that she was sorry, and she would be right there. I hung up the phone and sat there bawling my eyes out. I did not know what to say to my mom once I saw her. It's been two years. I decided to sleep until it was time to push. I felt a hand lightly stroking my face. I opened up my eyes, and there was my mom. I smiled at her, and she smiled back. Then the doctor came in and checked me. She told me that I was doing good, and it should be about another two hours.

So my mom started asking me questions, and I sat there trying not to cry and answer them. She told me that she and my dad got into a big fight after I left, and he took off, never to be seen again. I held my hand over my mouth and let out a loud sigh. I asked about my little brother. She answered that he was at the babysitter's house. I was so relieved that I started to feel a little better.

Then she asked the million-dollar question, "Who was the father of the baby?"

Tears ran down my face as I told her it's Dad. She had a look on her face as if she was not surprised. Then she asked if I was going to keep the baby. I quickly told her no.

I suddenly screamed, "Help me!"

The nurse came in and asked me what was wrong. I told her that I was in a lot of pain and I felt a lot of pressure down there. She checked me and said that it was time; the baby was on its way. I pushed for about an hour, and finally, the baby was here. The nurse announced that it was a healthy baby girl. I smiled and asked if I could see her. The nurse brought her to me, and when I looked at her, I was amazed at how beautiful she was. I thought about the decision I had made and wondered if I had made the right decision.

I started to cry, and my mom came rushing to me. I told her that I might want to keep the baby, and my mom smiled and said, "That's your decision, and whatever you decide, I am always going to be there for you no matter what."

I felt like a burden had been lifted when my mom said that. I told the nurse to hold off the adoption and give me some time to think about it.

The day grew shorter, and night seemed longer. You tried to do more, but it seemed as if there was still not enough time in the day. People were walking and driving around as if they had no care in the world. No one really knows what the future holds for them, so they do all they can now so that their life seemed like it has a purpose.

I moved back home with my mom and little brother. Things are going great. I am back in school, doing good, and even have a few friends. I helped out around the house more, and my mom and I talked all the time now. The sky seemed brighter, and the clouds were moving slowly across the sky. I was happy for the first time in my life. As time went by, I got stronger and wiser. I saw things in a different light. After I graduated from high school, I decided to go to college and became an advocate for people who had been raped. I wanted to be the voice that they did not have and make the world less scary.

I saw my daughter on the weekends, and she was so beautiful and smart. I looked into her eyes and wondered what she would be thinking about. There is a whole world out here for her to explore, and if I have anything to do with it, she will.

Awaken from a dream to a nightmare
He grabs me without a care
With mouth muffed and willpower strained
He pierces me violently with horrible pain
And when it was over and he was done
He threatens me with fear then he was gone
Now I lay shaken with fright
I knew I never forget that night

Runaway

The storm came through like a werewolf howling as the leaves on the trees gave in. Nobody was on the streets; it was as quiet as waves on a bright and sunny day. Hi, my name is Amy, and I am fourteen years old, and this is my story.

I lived in a three-bedroom house with my mom, my dad, and my grandparents on my mom and dad's side of the family. It was very crowded here, and if you were not careful, you would get trampled on. See, my mom and dad have ten kids, and they all have moved out there but me. It all started when I was twelve years old. My mom and dad were arguing about me. Mom said that I was a good child, and I was doing the best I could for my age. Then I heard my dad say that I was hardheaded and useless and could do better. I quietly put my hand over my mouth and backed away from the door and into my room. It stung like a bee, and my heart was racing very fast. I wondered what I had done for my dad to say that.

Then all of a sudden, my room door opened, and my dad was standing there in the doorway. He looked at me in disgust and started yelling at me, telling me that I was a waste of time and he wished I were not born. He stepped closer and slapped me, and then he turned around and left. I put my hand to my face as tears ran down. I don't know what I had done to deserve this type of abuse. My mom came in about twenty minutes later to see if I was okay.

Then all of a sudden, I could hear my dad yelling to my mom, "Leave that brat alone! She deserves what she got!"

My mom slowly turned away and left me there crying. I got on my knees and prayed for something good to happen so I would not feel this pain that I felt inside. I decided that I was not going to be this weak little person. So I packed up what I could take in my book bag and left throughout the window. I did not know where I was going or what to do. But I knew I could not stay there at that moment.

I walked downtown where all the homeless people were. I found myself a seat and sat down to rest. I realized that I had not eaten and was getting very hungry. I looked around to see if I could find someone who would help me. The first couple I approached looked at me like garbage and kept walking. I realized that this was not going to be easy. So I sat down and thought of a way to get something to eat. I must have fallen asleep because when I woke up, it was already the next day. I got up and walked down the street looking for a place to eat. I ran across this restaurant that sold Chinese food. I went inside and asked for the manager. She came out, and I asked her if I could do the dishes for exchange of food. She looked me over and said yes. She then took my hand and led me to the kitchen and told me to sit. She left and came back with a bowl of soup, chicken, and soda. I thanked her and started to eat.

When I was done, I carried my bowl over to the dishwasher, and I did every dish there was to do. I felt weird, but it was a deal. When I was finished, I went and found the manager to let her know that I was done. She went to see my work and said that I've done more than her regular employees. We laughed, and I started to turn away, and the manager stopped me. She offered me a job, and she gave me some money. I was shocked and did not know what to say. I agreed and left the restaurant with pride and dignity. Well, this lasted for about three months. I saved the money she gave me just for the rainy day. I started to miss home, and I really wanted to go back, and that's what I did—I went home. Since I did not have a TV to watch, I did not know that my parents were looking for me. When I entered the door, everyone rushed to me, all talking at once. I kept saying that I was okay and I was sorry for running away.

Well, I wish I could tell you that it got better, but it didn't. If it was not my dad striking me and yelling me, it was his parents. My mom and her parents tried to save me, but it was no use. They would trip me when I walked by and laugh when I fell. They would hit me just because and told me that I was not wanted. Every time my mom and her parents would try to intervene, it made them treat me even worse than before. So I tried to stay away from them, but that was not easy at all. It got to the point that they would hurt me so bad that one day they broke my arm. My mom got mad at them and told them that it had to stop. She then took me to the emergency room.

When we got there, it was crowded, and it seemed like a long wait. We checked in, and they took us right at back. The doctor came in and examined my arm. He then sent me to go get x-rays to see if it was broken. When the doctor came back, he said that it was broken and that I would have to have a cast on. I sighed and said okay. The doctor started to leave but turned around and looked at me and asked me how it happened. Tears started falling down my face as I looked at my mom. She got up from her chair and stood next to me and said that I fell while playing outside. The doctor shook his head and said that kids will be kids as he headed out of the room.

My mom then put her arms around me and said that everything would be okay. By the time we got home, everyone was resting on the couch watching TV. They all looked at me and said, "Poor baby, are you okay?" Mom said that I was just fine and it's just a broken arm. She led me in the kitchen and fixed us something to eat. After I finished eating, I went to my room and went to sleep. I thought of myself having a cast on my arm and how they were the cause of it and that things would be better. But I was wrong, my dad and mom would still be arguing, and mostly it would be about me. He would still call me out of my name and, in disgust, wished that I were not born. My dad's parents would say nasty things to me while my mom and her parents came to my aid. This went on for about two years.

I was in and out of the hospital; it seemed like once every month, something was broken in me. I started to hate my life and wished that I was dead. But the final straw was when my dad beat me for no good reason and his parents stayed there and held me down while he did it. My dad hit me so hard that he knocked me unconscious. As a lay there lifeless, my mom came in there and fired a shot in the air. Everyone stopped what they were doing and looked at her with disbelief. My dad asked my mom if she had lost her mind, and she said yes and that if he did not stop, he was going to lose his. She ran over to where I was lying and called for me, but there was no answer. She hurried up and called for help while tears ran down her face. I guess my mom was fed up and did not care anymore, but one thing's for sure: she was not going to let them hurt me anymore.

She stood over my body until the emergency crew came, and they hauled me away quickly. While in the ambulance, I quit breathing, and they had to do CPR to bring me back. My mom was at the back of the ambulance with me crying and saying sorry to me. When we got to the hospital, they rushed me right in, hooking me up to all kinds of machines. The doctors that were helping were in shock when they removed my clothes. Nobody could have been prepared for what they saw next. I was covered in bruises from the top of my head to the bottom of my feet. The doctors all stepped back and wondered what type of person would do this to a kid. One of the doctors got on the phone, and I already knew whom she was on the phone with.

A couple of hours later, the lady showed up from the Child Protective Services asking me a lot of questions. My mom just sat there quietly, not saying a word. So I told the lady everything that has been happening to me since I was twelve. The lady had tears in her eyes; she just could not believe that someone could do this to a child. The CPS lady went to talk to my mom, but she was not trying to hear what the lady had to say.

My mom kept on yelling, "You are not going to take her!"

I looked at both the lady and my mom and yelled, "I am not going back to that house with you!" Tears started falling down my face, so I got up and put my clothes on and left. My mom and the CPS lady were calling for me to come back, but I just kept on walking. I walked around until I could not walk anymore. I went to the restaurant that I had been working at to sit and to think about my next move. My boss saw me and came over to see if I needed anything. I told her that I needed a permanent place to stay and something to eat. My boss said that she had an apartment upstairs right above the restaurant and that I could stay there for as long as I needed to. I thanked my boss and took the key and went upstairs to my new place.

It was my first apartment, and I was very excited but also scared. I had never lived on my own, and there was no one there but me. The apartment was furnished, and it had a little food in the cabinet and refrigerator. I went downstairs and asked my boss for something to eat. Once I got my food, I went back upstairs and ate in silence. I cleaned up the mess I made and went to sleep. I woke up the next morning, and still nobody was there but me. I decided to watch TV. I turned on the news to see that our house was surrounded by cop cars. I sat there in disbelief, not knowing what was going on. I wanted to call my mom to find out, but just as I picked up the receiver, I saw my mom in handcuffs being walked to the squad car. Tears ran fast down on my face. I wanted to save her, but I realized that she did not save me. As I continued to watch, one by one, everyone that lived in the house was brought out in handcuffs. I was a little relieved to see my dad and his parents detained. That meant that they could not hurt me anymore. I turned the TV off and sat in silence for a while.

The next day, I decided that I wanted more out of my life than what I was dealing. So I decided to go back to school and worked part-time to have money for clothes. I did this for the next four years of my life. I finished school with high honors and decided that after graduation, I wanted a new scenery. After I crossed the stage, I went and bought a one-way ticket to Las Vegas. I said goodbye to my boss at the restaurant. I went by the house to say goodbye to my mom, but nobody was at home. I caught the bus to the airport and waited until my flight was called.

As I entered the doors of the plane, I heard someone calling my name. I looked back, and it was my mom. She was walking toward me quickly. I stopped and walked back toward her to see why she was here. She looked at me with tears running down her face. She said that she was very sorry for everything that had happened to me and wanted me to forgive her. I said nothing to her, turned around, and boarded the plane. I wanted to forgive my mom, but how could I? I sat in my seat as the plane took off, and I cried. But then I thought, *Why should I cry when I have a new life ahead of me where nobody can hurt me again?* I put my headphones in my ear and sat back while I enjoyed the flight to freedom.

I see it coming all too slow
I see it coming with such a powerful blow
Can't run for cover nowhere to hide
I wait until they're all sleep inside
And pack my bags and hit the streets
It's scary out here nobody to see
But it's better than them beating on me
My mind on freedom and a better life
Far away from all this misery and strife

About the Author

*S*onja Slack is married with one child and one grandchild. She was born in Chicago, Illinois, and raised in Champaign, Illinois. She moved to Indianapolis in 2010. She has had odd jobs all her life, but she was very good at writing short stories. In 2018, she wrote her first book of three short stories. She has more short stories to come.

Printed in the United States
By Bookmasters